THE GREAT
BIG
BOOK
OF READING
PRESCHOOL

A NEW BURLINGTON BOOK
The Old Brewery
6 Blundell Street
London N7 9BH

Conceived, edited and designed by
QED Publishing
A Quarto Group Company
226 City Road
London EC1V 2TT
www.qed-publishing.co.uk

ISBN 978 1 84835 116 5

Publisher: Steve Evans
Creative Director: Zeta Davies

Printed and bound in China

THE GREAT
BIG
BOOK
OF READING
PRESCHOOL

NEW
BURLINGTON
BOOKS

Contents

When I'm a Grown-up

Anne Faundez

Illustrated by Katherine Lucas

When I'm a grown-up,
Who will I be?

A bird in the air,

Or a fish in the sea?

When I'm a grown-up,
What will I do?

Fly a spaceship to Mars,
Or work in a zoo?

11

When I'm a grown-up,
Will I be tall?

Huge like a hippo,

Or round like a ball?

When I'm a grown-up, what will I eat?

14

Pineapple pie, or some other treat?

15

When I'm a grown-up,

16

Who will live with me?

A frog or a dog?

Or a hoppity flea?

19

When I'm a grown-up, what will I wear?

 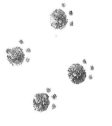  

Hmm, let me see, I really don't care!

When I'm a grown-up,
Will I travel by car?

Ride on a rhino,

Or swing from a star?

23

When I'm a grown-up,
I really don't mind
Who I will be...

As long as

I'm

ME!

Sing a Song of Sixpence

Compiled by Anne Faundez
Illustrated by Simone Abel

Sing a Song of Sixpence

Sing a song of sixpence,
A pocket full of rye,
Four and twenty blackbirds
Baked in a pie.

When the pie was opened,
The birds began to sing,
Wasn't that a dainty dish
To set before the king?

The king was in his counting house,
Counting out his money,
The queen was in the parlor,
Eating bread and honey.

The maid was in the garden,
Hanging out the clothes,
There came a little blackbird
And snapped off her nose.

Little Jack Horner

Little Jack Horner sat in a corner
Eating his Christmas pie,
He put in his thumb and pulled out a plum,
And said what a good boy am I!

Little Miss Muffet

Little Miss Muffet
Sat on a tuffet,
Eating her curds and whey.
Along came a spider
Who sat down beside her,
And frightened Miss Muffet away.

Here We Go 'Round the Mulberry Bush

Here we go 'round
   the mulberry bush,
The mulberry bush,
   the mulberry bush,
Here we go 'round
   the mulberry bush,
On a cold and
   frosty morning.

This is the way we
   wash our hands,
Wash our hands,
   wash our hands,
This is the way we
   wash our hands,
On a cold and
   frosty morning.

This is the way we
   brush our teeth,
Brush our teeth,
   brush our teeth,
This is the way we
   brush our teeth,
On a cold and
   frosty morning.

This is the way we
   go to school,
Go to school,
   go to school,
This is the way we
   go to school,
On a cold and
   frosty morning.

One, Two, Three, Four, Five

One, two, three, four, five,
Once I caught a fish alive.
Six, seven, eight, nine, ten,
Then I let it go again.

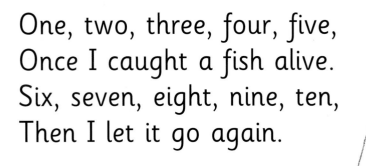

Why did you let it go?
Because it bit my finger so.
Which finger did it bite?
This little finger on the right.

Two Little Dicky Birds

Two little dicky birds
Sitting on a wall,
One named Peter,
One named Paul.

Fly away, Peter!
Fly away, Paul!
Come back, Peter!
Come back, Paul!

Old King Cole

Old King Cole
Was a merry old soul,
And a merry old soul was he.
He called for his pipe and
He called for his bowl,
And he called for his fiddlers three.

Cock a Doodle Doo!

Cock a doodle doo!
My dame has lost her shoe,
My master's lost his fiddling stick,
And doesn't know what to do.

Hush, Little Baby

Hush, little baby, don't say a word,
Mama's going to buy you a mocking-bird.

And if that mocking-bird don't sing,
Mama's going to buy you a diamond ring.

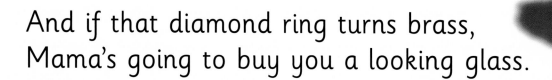

And if that diamond ring turns brass,
Mama's going to buy you a looking glass.

And if that looking glass gets broke,
Mama's going to buy you a billy goat.

And if that billy goat won't pull,
Mama's going to buy you a cart and bull.

And if that cart and bull turn over,
Mama's going to buy you a dog
named Rover.

And if that dog named
   Rover won't bark,
Mama's going to buy you
   a horse and cart.

And if that horse and cart fall down,
You'll still be the sweetest little baby
   in town.

Girls and Boys Come Out to Play

Girls and boys come out to play,
The moon doth shine as bright as day,
Leave your supper and leave your sleep,
And join your playfellows in the street.
Come with a hoop, come with a call,
Come and be merry, or not at all,
Up the ladder and over the wall,
A penny loaf will serve us all.

Wee Willie Winkie

Wee Willie Winkie
Runs through the town,
Upstairs and downstairs
In his nightgown,
Rapping at the window,
Crying through the lock,
Are the children in their beds,
For it's now eight o'clock?

41

Hush-a-bye, Baby

Hush-a-bye, baby, on the tree top,
When the wind blows, the cradle will rock.
When the bough breaks, the cradle will fall,
And down will come baby, cradle, and all.

Sleep, Baby, Sleep

Sleep, baby, sleep!
Thy father watches the sheep,
Thy mother is shaking the dreamland tree,
And down falls a little dream on thee.
Sleep, baby, sleep!

Said Mouse
to Mole

Clare Bevan

Illustrated by Sanja Rescek

Said Mouse to Mole,
"How do you do?"

Said Mole to Mouse,
"And how are you?"

Said Mouse, "I'm feeling
sad and blue."

Said Mole, "I'm
feeling gloomy, too."

Said Mouse, "I wish that I could fly,
Like Bee and Bird across the sky."

Said Mole, "But if you fly around,
I'll miss you when I'm underground."

Said Mole, "I wish
that I could run,
Like Squirrel in the
summer sun."

50

Said Mouse, "But if you play outside, I'll miss you when I have to hide."

Said Mouse, "I wish that I could float,
Like Beetle in his sailboat."

Said Mole, "But if you sail away,
Who will talk to me all day?"

Said Mole, "I wish that I could sing,
Like Blackbird with his glossy wing."

Said Mouse, "But if you sing and shout,
The Big Bad Cat will prowl about!"

Said Mouse, "I wish that I could shine,
Like sunbeams in the summertime."

Said Mole, "But if
    you're shiny bright,
The Big Bad Cat will
    prowl all night."

57

Said Mole, "I wish that I could be
Taller than the tallest tree."

Said Mouse, "But if you grow so tall,
Your little house will be too small."

Said Mouse, "I wish that I could change
To something beautiful and strange."

Said Mole, "But if you're strange and new,
Will you like me? Will I like you?"

Said Mouse to Mole, said Mole to Mouse,
"Don't leave your home. Don't leave your house.
Don't be a snail. Don't be a star...

I LIKE YOU JUST THE WAY YOU ARE!"

Wait for Me!

Written and Illustrated
by Eileen Browne

"I'm thirsty and hot,"
said Eddie the elephant.

"Me too," said Piper
the parrot.

"So am I," said
    Slippy the snake.

"I've got an idea!" said Molly the monkey.
"Let's go to the cool, sparkly river."

"Hooray!" said everybody.

"But how do we get to the cool, sparkly river?"
asked Eddie the elephant.

67

"It's easy!" said Piper and Slippy and Molly.
"We cross the wide, sandy desert,
get past the huge pile of rocks,
push through the dark, tangled jungle,
and go over the green, slimy swamp.
That's how we get to the cool, sparkly river."

"Come on, follow us!"

They went to the wide, sandy desert.

"How can we cross it?"
asked Eddie the elephant.

"With a flap of my wings!" said Piper.

"With a slither and a zigzag,"
said Slippy.

"With a hop and
a skip," said Molly.

"Let's go!"

Stomp, stomp, stompety-stomp,
went Eddie the elephant.

"Wait for me!"

They reached the huge pile of rocks.

"How can we get past them?" asked Eddie.

"With a flap and a hop," said Piper.

"With a wiggle and a squeeze,"
said Slippy.

"With a scramble and a climb," said Molly.

Puff-pant, puff-pant, went Eddie.

"Wait for me!"

They came to the dark, tangled jungle.

"How can we get through it?" asked Eddie.

"With a flutter and a flap," said Piper.

"With a weave and a waggle," said Slippy.

"With a swing and a leap," said Molly.

Crash, smash, bumpity-bash, went Eddie.

"Wait for me!"

They got to the green, slimy swamp.

"How can we go over it?" asked Eddie.

"With a flap and a glide," said Piper.

76

"With a slither and a wriggle," said Slippy.

"With a run and a slide," said Molly.

Squish, squelch, splatter, and splash, went Eddie.

"Wait for me!"

At last, they arrived at the cool, sparkly river.

"Shall we fly in?" said Piper the parrot.

"Shall we slip in?" said Slippy the snake.

"Shall we climb in?" said Molly the monkey.

"Go in how you like... I'm JUMPING," said Eddie.

And Piper and Slippy and Molly all shouted,

"Hey! Wait for me!"

Teddy's Birthday

Written by Anne Faundez
Illustrated by Karen Sapp

The toys are up early. What's happening today?
They bump and they bounce; they're ready to play.

Now they are gathered, it's time for some fun.
It's Teddy's birthday; today he is ONE!

"It's my BIRTHDAY!" cries Teddy,
"I hope everyone's ready!

It's party-time soon,
Let's decorate the room!"

Balloons all around, flowers everywhere,
A banner on the wall, streamers in the air.

"Oh, wow!" says Teddy.
"Party now! Are you ready?"

They share out the hats in blue, green, and red.
Teddy takes TWO to put on his head!

"Let's play some games," say the Twin Yellow Bears.
So they play pass-the-package and musical chairs.

They clap to the music and make lots of noise,
Big Bear, Brown Bear—all of the toys.

Amanda the Panda and Jimmy Giraffe,
Together they dance and soon start to laugh.

Fluffy the Bunny has made lots of treats,
Cookies and buns, ice cream and sweets.

Everyone's hungry. They each find a seat.
With tummies a-rumbling, they tuck in and eat.

Next, there's a cake on a big silver dish.
Teddy blows hard, and then makes a wish.

The toys clap their hands and together start singing.
Teddy is happy and cannot stop grinning.

"Happy Birthday to you,
Happy Birthday to you!
Happy Birthday, dear Teddy!
Happy Birthday to you!"

There's a gift for Teddy.
He's very excited.
A new bouncy ball!
He's truly delighted!

The toys are now yawning. Such sleepyheads!
They put on pajamas and climb into bed.

After such an exciting and busy, busy day,
They close their eyes
And fall asleep...
right away.

Lenny's Lost Spots

Written by Celia Warren
Illustrated by Genny Haines

Lenny was a ladybug.
He was red with black spots.

In the morning, Lenny counted his spots:
One, two, three, four, five, six.

But in the afternoon, Lenny said,
"Where are my spots?
Where have they gone?
This morning I had six
but now I have none."

Lenny looked once.
Lenny looked twice.
He thought his spots
were on some dice.
But he was wrong.

Lenny looked down.
Lenny looked up.
He thought his spots
were on a pup.
But he was wrong.

Lenny looked high.
Lenny looked low.

He thought his spots were on a bow.
But he was wrong.

Lenny looked here.
Lenny looked there.
He thought his spots
were on a chair.
But he was wrong.

Lenny looked near.
Lenny looked far.
He thought his spots
were on a car.
But he was wrong.

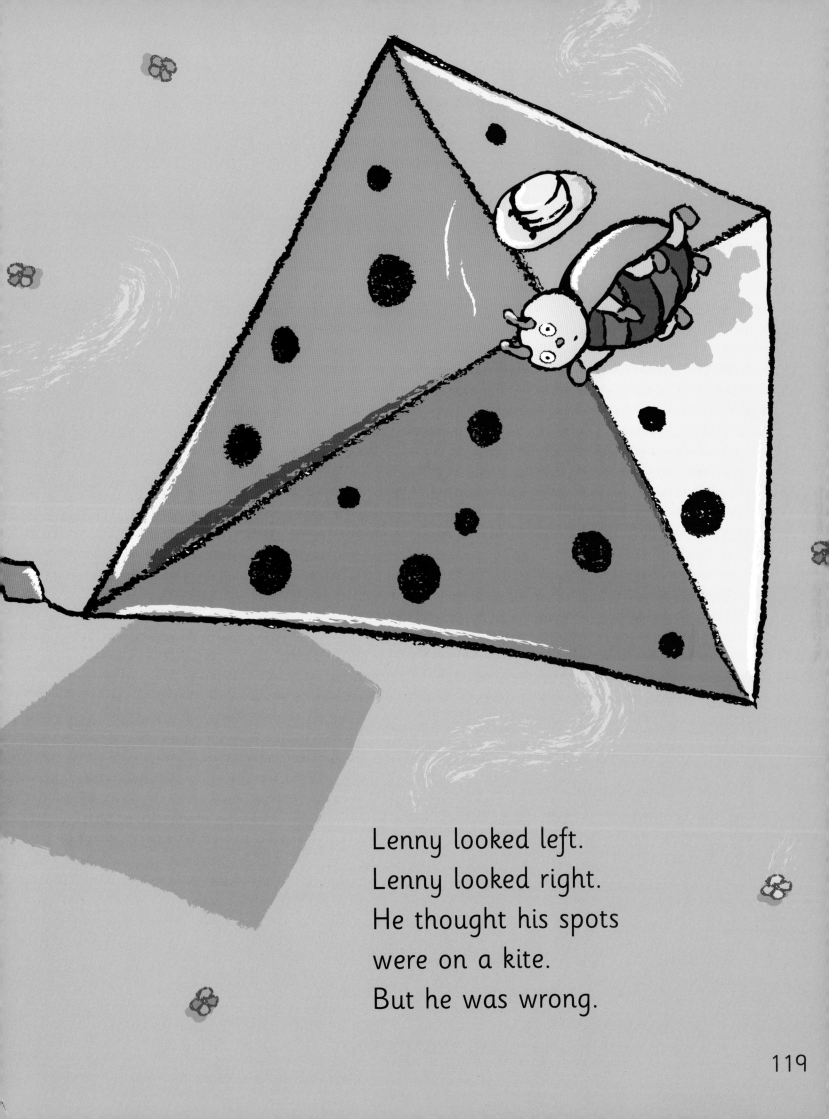

Lenny looked left.
Lenny looked right.
He thought his spots
were on a kite.
But he was wrong.

Lenny went out in the rain.
He said, "My spots are back again."

And he was right.

A Cloak for Swallow

Written by Anne Faundez
Illustrated by Adam Relf

Swallow shivered.
He had to fly away.
He should've left
weeks ago, but
he was having so
much fun with
his friends.

And now snowflakes,
soft as cotton, were
tumbling from the sky.

"It's too cold here," he cried.
"I must leave early tomorrow.
I'll wish my friends goodbye, and
then prepare for my journey."

"Owl! I must fly away before the snow sets in," Swallow said.

"Why don't you shelter in your nest until spring?" asked Owl.

"I'll be even colder when my nest turns to ice," replied Swallow.

Owl was silent.

"Say goodbye to everyone for me," said Swallow. "I'll see you all again next spring."

127

Owl knew Swallow should have left weeks ago.
The snowstorms would make his journey long
and difficult.

Owl hugged Swallow goodbye.
He was worried about Swallow.
Very worried.

Suddenly, Owl had
an idea, and went
to find his friends.

Owl called a meeting of the birds.
"We must help Swallow," he said.

"How?" said Magpie.

"We could make a
cloak to keep him warm
on his journey," said Owl.

The birds fluttered in excitement.

Just at that moment, Moon was on her way up the sky. She paused and listened to the birds.

"We'll finish by dawn," said Swan, "if we start now."

"We'll have to work all night," said Kingfisher.

So that's what they did.

They gathered some feathers and began
to weave them together, in and out,
in and out. They worked on and on,
weaving and winding.

And Moon shone down and gave them light.

Soon, the birds were too tired to go on.
They looked down at the bundle of feathers.

"We still haven't finished and
Swallow leaves tomorrow," cried Robin.

"We'll finish tomorrow, early, before Swallow leaves," yawned Kingfisher.

So the birds went home, tired and disappointed.

"The birds worked hard," said Moon,
"but there's still lots to do."

She sprinkled moonbeams
and began to weave
them, in and out,
in and out.

She worked until
dawn, weaving
and winding.

The birds woke early.

What a surprise!
The cloak was
ready—and
it was shimmering
with silver threads!

Owl smiled up at
Moon, as she slipped
down the sky.
"I also wish Swallow
a safe journey," said
Moon softly.

137

The birds rushed to Swallow's nest.

"Look, Swallow! We've made you a cloak.
And Moon helped, too. Put it on.
It will keep you warm when you
fly," said Owl excitedly.

Swallow hugged his friends as the snow began to fall.

"Thank you! I'll see you next year," he said.

And Swallow set off on his journey, warm and happy.

One, Two, Buckle My Shoe

Compiled by Anne Faundez

Illustrated by Brett Hudson

Hickory dickory dock,
The mouse ran up the clock.
The clock struck one,
The mouse ran down,
Hickory dickory dock.

Incy Wincy spider
Climbed up the water spout.
Down came the rain
And washed the spider out.
Out came the sun
And dried up all the rain,
And Incy Wincy spider
Climbed up the spout again.

Higgledy, piggledy, pop!
The dog has eaten
   the mop;
The pig's in a hurry,
The cat's in a flurry,
Higgledy, piggledy, pop!

144

Oh, the grand old Duke of York,
He had ten thousand men,
He marched them up to the top of the hill,
And he marched them down again.

And when they were up,
    they were up,
And when they were down,
    they were down,
And when they were
    only halfway up,
They were neither up nor down.

If you're happy and you know it,
Clap your hands;
If you're happy and you know it,
Clap your hands;
If you're happy and you know it
And you really want to show it,
If you're happy and you know it,
Clap your hands.

If you're happy and you know it,
Stamp your feet;
If you're happy and you know it,
Stamp your feet;
If you're happy and you know it
And you really want to show it,
If you're happy and you know it,
Stamp your feet.

I'm a little teapot, short and stout,
Here's my handle, here's my spout.
When I see the teacups, hear me shout,
Tip me over and pour me out!

Mary, Mary, quite contrary,
How does your garden grow?
With silver bells and cockleshells,
And pretty maids all in a row.

Hey, diddle, diddle,
The cat and the fiddle,
The cow jumped over
   the moon,
The little dog laughed
To see such sport,
And the dish ran away
   with the spoon.

150

Humpty Dumpty sat on a wall,
Humpty Dumpty had a great fall.
All the king's horses and all the king's men
Couldn't put Humpty together again.

Old MacDonald had a farm,
E-I-E-I-O!

And on that farm he had some pigs,
E-I-E-I-O!

With an oink oink here
and an oink oink there
here an oink
there an oink
everywhere an oink, oink!

Old MacDonald had a farm,
E-I-E-I-O!

And on that farm he had some ducks,
E-I-E-I-O!

With a quack quack here
and a quack quack there
here a quack
there a quack
everywhere a quack,
quack!

Old MacDonald had a farm,
E-I-E-I-O!

I had a little nut tree
And nothing would it bear
But a silver nutmeg and a golden pear.

The King of Spain's daughter came to visit me,
And all for the sake of my little nut tree.

I skipped over water, I danced over sea,
And all the birds in the air couldn't catch me.

The Queen of Hearts
She made some tarts,
All on a summer's day.
The Knave of Hearts
He stole those tarts,
And took them clean away.

Old Mother Hubbard
Went to the cupboard,
To give her poor dog a bone;
But when she got there,
The cupboard was bare
And so the poor dog had none.

She went to the store
To buy him some fruit;
But when she came back,
He was playing the flute.

She went to the hatter's
To buy him a hat;
But when she came back,
He was feeding the cat.

The dame made a curtsy,
The dog made a bow,
The dame said, "Your servant."
The dog said, "Bow-wow."

One, two, buckle my shoe
Three, four, knock at the door
Five, six, pick up sticks
Seven, eight, lay them straight
Nine, ten,
A big fat hen!

Twinkle, twinkle little star,
How I wonder what you are.
Up above the world so high,
Like a diamond in the sky.
Twinkle, twinkle little star,
How I wonder what you are.

159

Index